MW01064267

The KidHaven Science Library

Light

by Bonnie Juettner

KIDHAVEN PRESS™

THOMSON

™

GALE

San Diego • Detroit • New York • San Francisco • Cleveland
New Haven, Conn. • Waterville, Maine • London • Munich

THOMSON
★ ™
GALE

© 2004 by KidHaven Press. KidHaven Press is an imprint of The Gale Group, Inc.,
a division of Thomson Learning, Inc.

KidHaven™ and Thomson Learning™ are trademarks used herein under license.

For more information, contact
KidHaven Press
27500 Drake Rd.
Farmington Hills, MI 48331-3535
Or you can visit our Internet site at http://www.gale.com

LIBRARY OF CONGRESS CATALOGING-IN-PUBLICATION DATA

Juettner, Bonnie.
    Light : by Bonnie Juettner.
        v. cm. — (The Kidhaven science library)
Includes bibliographical references and index.
Contents: What is light?—How light affects living things—Light's special effects—
Modern uses of light.
        ISBN 0-7377-2074-3 (lib. bdg. : alk. paper)
    1. Light—Juvenile literature. [1. Light.] I. Title. II. Series.
        QC360 .J84 2004
        535' .078—dc21

                                                                        2003011276

Printed in the United States of America

Gumdrop
11/06

Contents

Chapter 1

What Is Light?

Light is energy. It is a form of energy that can be seen. Light is the only form of energy people can can see. In fact, light is the only thing that people can see. When people think they see the world around them, they are actually seeing the light bouncing off objects in their environment. Scientists know a lot about light, but they do not know exactly what light is. They have had to learn about light by observing how it behaves.

Speed of Light

One of the first things scientists tried to observe about light was its speed. In the 1600s, the Italian astronomer Galileo tried to measure the speed of light. He and an assistant went to the tops of two hills, which were a mile apart. They each had a covered lantern. Galileo uncovered his lantern. His assistant was to uncover his own lantern as soon as he saw the light from Galileo's lantern. Galileo intended to note the difference between the time when he uncovered his lantern and the time when he saw the light from his assistant's lantern. Unfortunately for Galileo, light travels very fast. It travels so fast that he could see the light from his assistant's lantern before he had a chance to note how much time had passed. What Galileo really needed was two hills that were very far

Galileo (right) discusses his research with his assistant. The two tried to measure the speed of light two hundred years before it was accurately calculated.

apart, perhaps as far apart as Earth and the Sun. Light takes eight minutes to travel from the Sun to Earth. But it was not possible for Galileo to send his assistant off the planet.

In the 1800s, James Maxwell, a Scottish scientist, also wondered about the speed of light. He knew that energy cannot be created or destroyed. Energy can only be changed from one form into another. (For example, burning coal changes stored chemical energy in the coal into another form, heat.) So if light were ever to slow down, he reasoned, it would get slower and slower and eventually stop. Its energy would be lost (or destroyed). If light were ever to speed up, it would grow stronger and stronger. This would be the same as creating energy. Maxwell knew neither of these things could happen. He was left with only one possibility. Light must travel at one speed. Using mathematical equations based on experiments he had done with electricity and magnetism, he calculated what the speed of light must be. He determined that light travels at about 186,000 miles (or 300,000 kilometers) per second.

Maxwell's calculations were correct. Light does travel that fast. In fact, scientists do not know of anything that can travel faster.

Straight Lines

As Galileo discovered, it is not always easy to do experiments with light. Scientists have had to learn much of what they know about light the way Maxwell did, by observing how light behaves and then thinking about what they know. This is how scientists figured out that light travels in straight lines. Observing shadows, they noted that light does not go around a solid object. Instead, the light is blocked, forming a shadow. From this, scientists deduced that light must travel in straight lines, which are often called rays. If light did not travel in a straight line, it could go around a solid object, and there would be no shadow.

Diffraction

Although light travels in straight lines, sometimes those lines bend. This is called **diffraction**. Scientists have observed diffraction, too, by looking at shadows. The edge of a shadow always looks a little blurry. That is because some light does diffract around solid objects. At first, this seemed contradictory to scientists. How could light travel in straight lines, but also move around an object in its path?

Scientists had to develop a special theory, called quantum mechanics, to explain this. According to this theory, light behaves as if it were made of particles but also as if it were made of a wave, like the waves in water. Traveling in straight lines, light is behaving more like a particle. But when light diffracts around objects, it is behaving more like a wave. For example, if a ball rolls along the ground and hits a rock, it will bounce off the rock. It will not go around the rock and continue on its original path. But if a stream of water hits a rock, it does not bounce off. Instead, it flows around the rock. Light behaves like the stream and the ball, at the same time. Light does bounce off solid objects. But it also diffracts around them.

Reflection

At first scientists thought it was impossible for light to do both. Then they realized that if light was behaving this way, it must be possible. So they revised their theories.

But if some light diffracts around objects, while most light is blocked and creates a shadow, this raises another question. What happens to the light rays that do not diffract around an object? There are several possibilities. If the object is transparent, like air or glass, light can travel right through it. If the object is opaque—as a person's body is—it will not allow light to travel through. Instead, the object will **reflect** light, but not all light. It absorbs the rest. Some objects, like mirrors, reflect light uniformly in all directions. The light rays hit the mirror and bounce off. That is why people can see themselves when they look in a mirror. The light reflecting off the person's body hits the mirror and bounces off again.

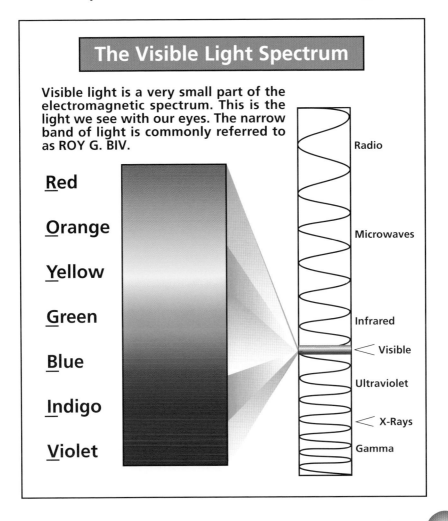

The Visible Light Spectrum

Visible light is a very small part of the electromagnetic spectrum. This is the light we see with our eyes. The narrow band of light is commonly referred to as ROY G. BIV.

<u>R</u>ed

<u>O</u>range

<u>Y</u>ellow

<u>G</u>reen

<u>B</u>lue

<u>I</u>ndigo

<u>V</u>iolet

Radio

Microwaves

Infrared

Visible

Ultraviolet

X-Rays

Gamma

Electromagnetic Radiation

When light is reflected off an object, it is behaving like a particle. To understand how light travels, though, it is necessary to think about how light behaves like a wave. Waves that travel through a substance, such as water, produce ripples in the substance. Light waves do not need a substance to travel through, as water waves do, but light waves still produce ripples. They cause ripples in the invisible electric and magnetic fields that surround Earth. It can be hard to imagine electric and magnetic fields, since they cannot be seen. This is a lot like gravity. Earth's gravity forms a gravitational field around the whole planet. People cannot see Earth's gravitational field, but they can see its effects. For example, a ball that is dropped will fall to the ground, pulled there by Earth's gravity.

People can also see the effects of Earth's magnetic field. One way to do this is to use a compass. No matter which way the compass is turned, its needle will move to stay aligned with Earth's North and South Poles, which are magnetic poles. Like Earth, other planets, the stars, and even the Moon are surrounded by electric and magnetic fields.

Because light disturbs electric and magnetic fields, it is a kind of electromagnetic wave. There are many types of electromagnetic waves. Light is only one of these. Some others are radio waves, television waves, microwaves, heat, ultraviolet waves,

Gravity, an invisible force much like electromagnetic radiation, pulls roller coaster riders downward with great force.

X-rays, and gamma rays. Together, these waves make up the electromagnetic spectrum.

All electromagnetic waves travel at the same speed, the speed of light. But they travel at different frequencies. The **frequency** is the number of times

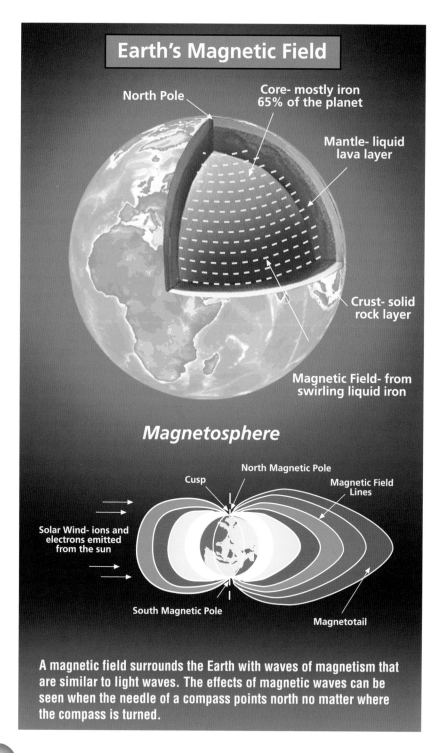

Earth's Magnetic Field

North Pole

Core- mostly iron 65% of the planet

Mantle- liquid lava layer

Crust- solid rock layer

Magnetic Field- from swirling liquid iron

Magnetosphere

Cusp

North Magnetic Pole

Magnetic Field Lines

Solar Wind- ions and electrons emitted from the sun

South Magnetic Pole

Magnetotail

A magnetic field surrounds the Earth with waves of magnetism that are similar to light waves. The effects of magnetic waves can be seen when the needle of a compass points north no matter where the compass is turned.

a wave crests in a particular unit of time. As the frequency of a wave gets higher, its wavelength, the distance from the top of one wave to the top of the next one, gets shorter. Higher frequency waves have shorter wavelengths. Lower frequency waves have longer wavelengths. These differences in frequency and wavelength are the reason people (and some animals) can see colors. Violet and blue light travel at higher frequencies, with shorter wavelengths. Red and orange light travel at lower frequencies, so their wavelengths are longer.

Although scientists do not fully understand light, they do know that light is critically important to humans and all other living things on Earth. Without light, people could not see at all. Human eyes work only because light stimulates special cells in the back of the eye. More importantly, however, without light and heat from the Sun, Earth's plants could not grow. In addition, the planet would be too cold for life to continue to exist. People on Earth owe everything they have to the Sun and its light.

Chapter 2

How Light Affects Living Things

When people think about what they need to live, they usually think of food, water, and shelter. Some people might mention air to breathe and energy for heating their homes. Very few people would mention light. But light from the Sun is the one thing humans need most in order to survive on Earth. Without light from the Sun, people would not have water, food, shelter, energy for heat, or even air to breathe. How can this be?

The light from the Sun plays a key role in the evaporation cycle on Earth. As the Sun heats up a body of water, it evaporates into the atmosphere (1), where it forms as clouds (2). As the clouds move over land, they mix with water transpired from ground

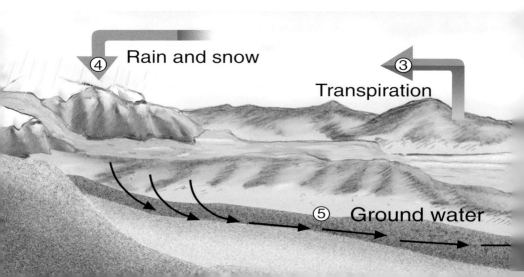

④ Rain and snow

③ Transpiration

⑤ Ground water

The Water Cycle

Humans can survive only a few days without water, and not just any water will do. Humans need fresh water to drink, not salt water. So they cannot drink water from Earth's oceans. Luckily, light from the Sun provides the energy for water to cycle from the oceans into the atmosphere, becoming clouds that then rain to make Earth's freshwater lakes, rivers, and underground water supply. How does this work?

Earth is constantly receiving **electromagnetic radiation** from the Sun. This radiation includes light that people can see, and heat. When the Sun's heat warms Earth's oceans, some water evaporates. It changes from a liquid into a vapor and rises into the atmosphere. The salt in the water, however, does not change into a vapor. It stays in the oceans.

cover (3). Eventually water from these clouds falls as rain or snow (4). The water that falls seeps into the ground becoming ground-water (5), where it moves through the rocks to the body of water (6) to start the cycle over again.

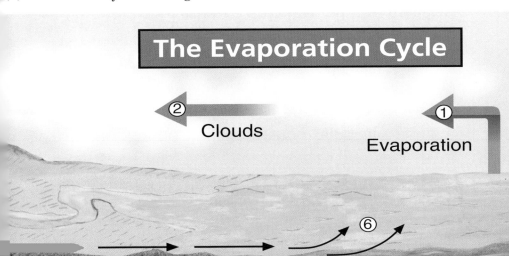

The Evaporation Cycle

② Clouds

① Evaporation

⑥

High in the atmosphere, the water vapor cools and forms clouds made of tiny droplets of water hanging in the air. Eventually, these clouds produce rain and snow. Some rain and snow falls back into the ocean. But much of it falls over land, producing Earth's rivers and lakes, and drips deep into the ground to replenish underground wells and reservoirs of water. This water supplies the fresh water that humans and other animals must drink in order to live.

How Plants Use Light

Like humans and other animals, plants need water. However, plants also use light to turn water and carbon dioxide into sugar. (Carbon dioxide is a gas that people and other animals exhale.) This is called **photosynthesis**. Most plants contain a green pigment called chlorophyll. Scientists do not know of any other substance besides chlorophyll that can capture light energy and convert it to chemical food energy. After converting light energy to chemical energy, plants can store it as sugar. Then they use the sugar to make foods. That way they can use the energy later, when they need it to grow new leaves or flowers.

People and other animals rely on plants to store energy from light because they can acquire that energy by eating parts of the plants. People also use plant materials to build houses, make clothing, produce medicines, and to burn as fuel. Many people around the world burn wood for heat, but people also get

How Photosynthesis Works

Chlorophyll in the plant absorbs light energy from the sun.

1

The leaves absorb carbon dioxide from the air.

2

The roots absorb water (3) and minerals and nutrients (4) from the ground.

3

4

The leaves give off oxygen and water vapors.

6

Light, carbon dioxide, water and nutrients are used to make sugars. The plant uses these sugars for food.

5

fossil fuels such as oil, coal, and natural gas from plants. These fuels were formed millions of years ago from the remains of dead plants and animals.

Because plants rely on photosynthesis to make food, they respond strongly to changes in light. If they get either too little or too much light, their leaves can turn yellow. Too much sun can cause a plant to get brown spots on its leaves, or drop some leaves. In addition, plants respond to seasonal changes in light. For example, deciduous trees drop their leaves in the fall when the days get shorter.

Plants Provide Oxygen

Although photosynthesis benefits humans and animals by providing food, it also provides another substance that is necessary for survival. That substance is oxygen. Plants release oxygen into the atmosphere during photosynthesis. Humans and other animals breathe in oxygen. Oxygen makes up only about one-fifth of Earth's air but without this oxygen people and animals could not survive. This is one reason why some people refer to rain forests as "Earth's lungs." The Amazon rain forest, for example, provides 20 to 30 percent of Earth's oxygen. If plants were unable to complete photosynthesis, eventually there would be almost no oxygen left in Earth's atmosphere. The only organisms that could survive on Earth, if that were the case, are a few types of bacteria that can live without converting light to food energy.

Sunbathers enjoy the beach and plenty of sunshine. Human skin is damaged from too much sun.

Other Reasons People Need Light

Like plants, humans respond to changes in light. When people are exposed to a lot of sunlight, their skin produces more melanin. Melanin is a pigment that can make lighter-skinned people look tan. It can also cause people to develop freckles, similar to the brown spots that plants get when they are exposed to too much sunlight. When humans are exposed to too much sunlight, however, they do not just freckle—they burn. The ultraviolet waves in sunlight, which are shorter and have a higher frequency than the rays of visible light, cause people to get sunburns.

However, too little light can produce health problems for humans too. Human skin can produce vitamin D if it is stimulated by sunlight. People need vitamin D to help regulate the amounts of calcium and phosphate in their bones. A lack of vitamin D can cause children to develop rickets, a

A man's nose is burned and infected from too much exposure to the sun.

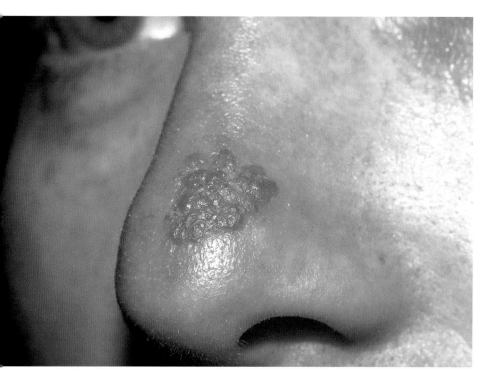

This young boy's legs are bowed from rickets. He developed the disease from a lack of vitamin D.

disease that causes bones to become soft or brittle. Adults who do not get enough vitamin D can develop osteomalacia, a disease that weakens the bones. Both rickets and osteomalacia can make it more likely for people to break their bones and to get cavities in their teeth. Children with rickets can develop bowlegs or curved spines. Fortunately, people who do not spend enough time in the sun can still

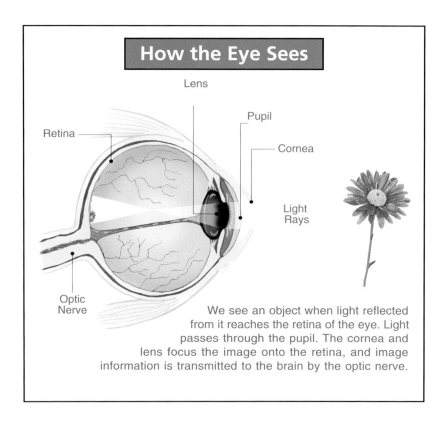

How the Eye Sees

Lens

Pupil

Retina

Cornea

Light Rays

Optic Nerve

We see an object when light reflected from it reaches the retina of the eye. Light passes through the pupil. The cornea and lens focus the image onto the retina, and image information is transmitted to the brain by the optic nerve.

get vitamin D from foods such as fish, dairy products, and eggs.

Even people who get enough vitamin D in their diets, however, can still suffer from lack of sunlight. Some people become depressed if they are not exposed to enough light. They develop a disorder called SAD, seasonal affective disorder, or winter depression. (Some people who are very sensitive to sunlight develop summer depression, another type of SAD, if they are exposed to too much light.) Scientists estimate that more than 5 percent of Americans develop SAD each winter. They theorize that SAD sufferers lose control of their natural body clock, which is controlled by a part of the brain. Doctors often treat patients with SAD by suggesting that they sit in front of a special light box every morning for thirty minutes. Some scientists think that light box therapy may also help patients who are suffering from other kinds of depression.

How the Eye Works

Of course, the most dramatic way light affects people is that it stimulates our eyes so that we can see. When light enters the human eye, it stimulates tiny antennae in the retina. The retina is the layer of tissue at the back of the eye. The retina's antennae are called rods and cones. Each human eye has millions of them. The cones allow people to see color. There are three types of cones, each sensitive to a different frequency, or different color, of light. The rods are sensitive only to lightness and darkness. Most mammals (including dogs and cats) have only rods in their eyes and thus can see only black, white, and shades of gray. Humans, primates (such as monkeys, apes, and lemurs), and a type of ground squirrel are the only mammals that can see color.

Humans may not always need to see colors in order to survive. But seeing colors does help people to enjoy art and appreciate nature. It also gives people the chance to view some of nature's most spectacular light displays—blue skies, sunsets, and even the light of fireflies.

Chapter 3

Light's Special Effects

Light does more than enable people to survive on Earth. Sometimes it also thrills and delights us.

Blue Skies and Sunsets

Some of light's most common effects can be seen simply by observing Earth's changing sky. On a clear day, the sky is blue. On cloudy or hazy days, the sky appears white or gray. At sunrise and sunset, the sky turns orange and red.

All colors of light are present in the light that Earth receives from the Sun. So all colors of light pass through Earth's atmosphere. But each color of light has a different wavelength. Violet light has the shortest wavelength. Red light has the longest wavelength. When each color passes through the atmosphere, it hits small particles of dust and molecules of nitrogen and oxygen that are in the air. When light with shorter wavelengths, such as violet and blue, hits a particle in the atmosphere, it reflects off the particle. This effect is known as scattering. Light with longer wavelengths, such as orange and red, does not scatter as much.

Because violet and blue light scatter so easily across the sky, it may be surprising that the sky does not look violet blue to people. However, people can see only light in wavelengths to which human eyes are sensitive. Humans can see all of the wavelengths of blue light but only a few of the wavelengths of violet light. So people can easily see all the shades of

A beautiful sunset reveals how red and orange light can travel long distances without scattering.

blue light that are scattered through the sky but can see only a few shades of violet. As a result, the sky looks more blue than violet to humans.

Light and the Atmosphere

On hazy or cloudy days, there are large droplets of water or particles of smoke in the air. These large particles reflect all light equally, no matter how long the wavelength is. When all colors are reflected equally, the result is white light. That is why clouds look white. Sometimes, however, the sky looks gray on days when there is a lot of pollution in the air or when clouds are especially thick and dense. In that case, some light is reflected, producing white light, but some light is blocked, producing shadows. The combination of the white light and shadows causes a gray effect.

But why does the sky turn orange and red at sunrise and sunset? At those times of day, when the sun is low on the horizon, sunlight must pass through more atmosphere to reach people's eyes. By the time the light reaches people's eyes, most blue light has already been scattered. But red and orange light can pass through long sections of atmosphere without being scattered. The red and orange light do not make the whole sky look red, though, because the sun is low in the sky and light travels in a straight line. So the area near the horizon looks red and orange, while the rest of the sky still looks blue. (Blue light also travels in a straight line, but

White light passes through tiny drops of water to form a rainbow.

through scattering, it bounces off one particle and then another until it fills the whole sky.)

There is one time when many colors appear in the sky at once—when sunlight passes through raindrops and forms a rainbow. This happens because raindrops do not absorb light, or reflect it across the sky. Instead, light passes through them. But when a wave of light passes through a raindrop, it bends and comes out at a different angle. Each wavelength of light bends at a particular angle, so each wavelength, or color, comes out at its own unique angle. As a result, one ray of white light is separated into a band of colors—a rainbow.

Firelight and Electric Light

The Sun is not Earth's only source of light. People can get light from electric lights, fires, and candles, for example. Although light from these sources does not come from the Sun, it is still a form of electromagnetic radiation, and it still travels in waves.

Light from a flame is called **incandescence**. This kind of light is produced when a substance becomes so hot that it begins to glow. Although the flames of a fire may look as though they do not contain any material substance, they actually do. They contain tiny particles of carbon. When carbon gets very hot, it begins to glow, and it is this glow that people can see when looking at a fire.

Most lightbulbs work the same way. The lightbulbs in most electric lamps, in car headlights, and in flashlights contain a piece of metal wire made of tungsten. Tungsten can get very hot without melting, and at high temperatures it gives off incandescent light. When a light switch is turned on, electricity flows into the wire and heats the tungsten. Light from the heated tungsten fills the room.

Some electric lights, however, are not incandescent but fluorescent. They do not rely on heat to produce light, so fluorescent lights are sometimes called "cool lamps." They give off a type of light

Electromagnetic radiation produces incandescent light from a campfire (below), a candle (center), and an electric light-bulb (top).

called **luminescence**. Luminescence is light that is given off when energy flows into a substance. In a fluorescent light tube, energy must travel through at least four different substances. First, electricity flows into a tungsten wire, just as it does in an incandescent lightbulb. But the tube is filled with mercury vapor and argon gas. Argon conducts electricity between the tungsten wire and the mercury vapor. This causes the atoms of mercury vapor to get excited and give off ultraviolet radiation. This radiation is absorbed by the coating on the inside of the tube, which begins to fluoresce and give off light.

Light Displays in Nature

Some living things can luminesce, or produce visible light similar to the light from a fluorescent lamp. This phenomenon is called **bioluminescence.** Most animals that can produce light live in the oceans. For example, many types of bacteria, fish, jellyfish, and squid can produce light. Very few land creatures can do so, but a few, such as fireflies, can. Scientists think that bioluminescence is useful for sea creatures that live so deep in the ocean that their environment includes little or no light. Some deep-sea animals release bioluminescent chemicals into the water to confuse a predator, giving them a chance to escape. Others use light displays to attract their own prey, or to attract a mate. Some have bioluminescent headlamps to help them see.

A jellyfish glows colorfully. Certain sea creatures produce light to attract prey, to help them see, or to confuse predators.

Like bioluminescent animals, some nonliving substances can give off light. Eggshells, ivory, and some gems and minerals can do this. However, in animals, light is given off when different chemicals in an animal's body react together. For a nonliving substance to luminesce, it must first be exposed to energy. Then it can give off light for a time after the energy source has been removed. This ability is called **phosphorescence**, or occasionally, afterglow.

These kangaroo rats glow from fluorescent powder. Scientists covered them with powder to prepare them for an experiment.

Toys that glow in the dark are made of phosphorescent materials. They must first be exposed to light, and then they can glow in the dark for a while, but not forever. Not all phosphorescent materials will glow after exposure to sunlight, though. Some must be stimulated by ultraviolet rays or X-rays, which contain more energy than visible light.

Light displays can be fun to look at, but scientists have discovered that they are also quite useful. Many tools that people rely on today, such as eyeglasses and computer monitors, were developed by inventors experimenting with light's ability to bend and reflect, or with the ability of certain substances to luminesce.

Chapter 4

Modern Uses of Light

Although scientists still do not fully understand light, they have invented many tools that use it. Most people use a few of these tools every day.

Tools That Work Like the Human Eye

Humans can see light because our eyes are sensitive to it. As scientists learn more about the way human eyes work, they have been able to invent tools to help people see better. The first part of the human eye that scientists tried to reproduce and use was the lens. Human eyes contain two lenses. When light enters a human eye, it must pass through these lenses, which focus and direct the light onto the retina at the back of the eye. There, the light stimulates cells that are sensitive to it, and the cells send a message to the brain.

The lens of a human eye can change its size and shape to focus light on the retina. This allows humans to look at objects that are near and at

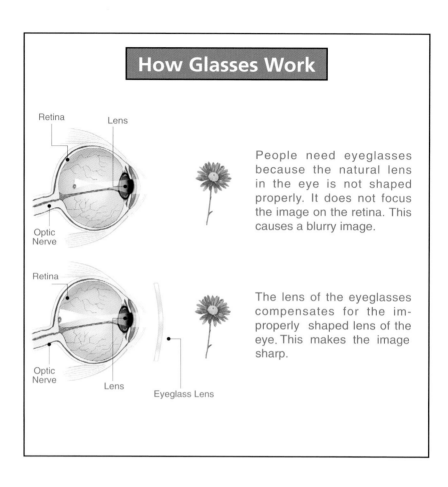

How Glasses Work

Retina   Lens

Optic Nerve

People need eyeglasses because the natural lens in the eye is not shaped properly. It does not focus the image on the retina. This causes a blurry image.

Retina

Optic Nerve   Lens   Eyeglass Lens

The lens of the eyeglasses compensates for the improperly shaped lens of the eye. This makes the image sharp.

objects that are far away. Some people, however, have lenses in their eyes that cannot adjust enough to allow them to see objects clearly if they are too far away or too close. Two thousand years ago, the Roman philosopher Seneca is said to have solved this problem by reading books through a glass globe filled with water. The glass and the water worked together to bend, or focus, the light on the way into his eyes.

After about the year 1000, scientists around the world had begun developing simple magnifying glasses. A magnifying glass bends light in such a way that it makes objects appear larger than they are. Over the course of the next two hundred years, scientists figured out how to make eyeglasses using lenses like those in magnifying glasses. Then, in the late 1500s, eyeglass makers Hans and Zacharias Janssen put two lenses together and developed the first microscope. Soon after that, another eyeglass maker, Hans Lippershey, invented the telescope.

Microscopes and telescopes are very much like each other. Both magnify images so that people can clearly see details that would otherwise be too

A little girl delights in a distant view through her telescope.

small for the human eye. But telescopes magnify images that are too small to see because they are reflections of objects that are far away. Microscopes magnify images that are too small to see because they come from light reflected off very tiny objects. Both use two lenses, one to gather light and one to magnify the image produced by the first lens. However, a telescope needs a very large lens, to gather as much light as possible from vast areas of sky. A microscope uses a much smaller lens.

As scientists worked with lenses, they also discovered ways to make simple cameras. A camera works like an artificial human eye. Like the eye, a camera uses a lens to focus light on light-sensitive material. However, a human eye focuses light on the retina, while the lens of a camera focuses light on film. But the film in a camera works like the cells in the retina of an eye. When light hits the cells of a retina, chemical changes occur. Because of those changes, an image is sent to the brain. When light hits film in a camera, chemical changes also occur, and an image is recorded.

Tools That Use Phosphorescence

The retina of a human eye contains three types of cells, which are sensitive to red, green, and blue wavelengths of light. In the last century, when scientists began to work with computers, they had to

A lab technician researches AIDS with the help of a high-powered microscope.

figure out a way to translate images from a computer into combinations of red, green, and blue, so that people could see their work on a computer monitor.

The first color computer monitors had screens that were coated on the inside with phosphorescent materials. The inside of this kind of computer monitor, called a cathode-ray tube, is coated with dots or stripes of red, green, and blue phosphors. A phosphor is a substance that absorbs energy and then emits light. A filament in the back of the monitor, like the wire filament in a lightbulb, is heated just enough to cause it to give off three streams of electrons. The streams of electrons stimulate the phosphors on the inside of the monitor, causing them to glow in combinations of red, green, and blue. These combinations form an image on the screen of the monitor. Most computer monitors and television screens still work this way. (Some, such as the flat-screen monitors in laptop computers, work differently.)

Lasers

Lasers are another tool that scientists developed as they learned more about how light works. A **laser** is a tool that can produce a kind of light that is very different from sunlight. Sunlight, like most other kinds of visible light, contains many colors because light usually includes several different wavelengths. But laser light has only one wavelength. Unlike other kinds of light, laser light does not diffract. This means that it does not bend or spread out, as light from a flashlight does. Instead, it forms a strong, concentrated beam of light. This beam can be made strong enough to be used as a cutting tool. Some lasers are strong enough to cut through steel, but others are very weak and are used only as pointing tools.

A scientist observes as a laser bounces from one mirror to another without diffraction.

When they are used as cutting tools, lasers are much more precise than metal saws or drills could be. Lasers can be used to make very tiny cuts or indentations in a material. So they can be used to record information from a computer onto a compact disc (CD) or digital video disc. Laser light records computer data by etching patterns of pits and bumps on

A scientist conducts an experiment using fiber-optic cables.

the surface of a CD. Later, a CD player with a laser in it must be used to decode the pits and bumps.

Fiber Optics

Not only can lasers be used to store information in a small space, as on a CD, but they can also be used to transmit information very quickly through **fiber-optic** cables. Fiber-optic cables are lined with a special coating that reflects light. Laser light can travel through the cables, reflecting from one side of the cable to the other, until it reaches its destination. Fiber-optic cables are especially useful for transmitting information because they can bend around corners. They can be used as phone lines, television cable lines, or to provide high-speed Internet connections. Doctors also use fiber-optic cables to look inside the human body. They can make a small incision and insert a tiny tube containing two bundles of cables. One bundle carries light into the body, and another carries reflected light out.

Much of what scientists now know about light and how it can be used was unknown even as recently as one hundred years ago. At that time, there were no computers, no televisions, and no CD players. In just a few years, science has radically changed the way people live their daily lives. And scientists are learning more about how light works all the time. How might new inventions change the way people live one hundred years from now? Only time will tell.

Glossary

bioluminescence: The ability of some living things to produce light.

diffraction: Light's ability to bend a little to go around corners, and to spread out to fill a room.

electromagnetic radiation: Waves that make up the electromagnetic spectrum and travel by disrupting electric and magnetic fields.

fiber optics: Technology that makes it possible for laser light to carry information through a cable.

frequency: The number of times a wave crests in a particular unit of time.

incandescence: Light that is produced when a substance becomes so hot that it begins to glow.

laser: A tool that emits a tightly focused beam of light that has only one wavelength and does not diffract.

luminescence: Light that is given off when energy flows into a substance.

phosphorescence: The ability of some substances to continue to luminesce even after an energy source has been removed.

photosynthesis: The process by which a plant converts light energy to food.

reflection: Light's ability to hit certain objects and bounce off.

Books

Isaac Asimov, *How Did We Find Out About Lasers?* New York: Walker, 1990. An overview of the history of laser development and the basics of the way lasers work. Includes a discussion of how lasers are used today and how they might be used in the future.

Roy Gallant, *Rainbows, Mirages and Sundogs: The Sky as a Source of Wonder.* New York: Macmillan, 1987. An overview of light's special effects, along with some experiments to try.

Michael Pollard, *The Light Bulb and How It Changed the World.* New York: Facts On File, 1995. A history of the development of the lightbulb.

Alvin Silverstein, Virginia Silverstein, and Laura Silverstein Nunn, *Photosynthesis.* Brookfield, CT: Twenty-First Century, 1998. A good reference on the basics of how photosynthesis works and how scientists learned about it.

Steve Tomecek, *Bouncing and Bending Light.* New York: Scientific American Books for Young Readers, 1995. A guide for readers who would like to learn about light by doing their own experiments. A good reference for readers interested in learning more about how scientists observe natural phenomena.

Robert Wood, *Physics for Kids: 49 Easy Experiments with Optics.* Blue Ridge Summit, PA: TAB Books, 1990. An introduction to the study of light through experiments. Teaches readers how to make optical tools such as kaleidoscopes, periscopes, prisms, and telescopes.

Websites

How Stuff Works (www.howstuffworks.com). This searchable database includes many entries explaining how light, vision, and tools that use light work.

Science Made Simple (www.sciencemadesimple. com). A good source of science projects and experiments, with answers to science questions asked by kids.

Index

Picture Credits

Cover Photo: © Danny Lehman/CORBIS
©James L. Amos/CORBIS, 32
©Archivo Iconografico, S.A./CORBIS, 5
©Lester V. Bergman/CORBIS, 20
COREL Corporation, 11, 19, 27, 29 (bottom)
©Laura Doss/CORBIS, 35
James King-Holmes/Photo Researchers, Inc., 40
Library of Congress, 7
©Lawrence Manning/CORBIS, 39
©OSF/Parks, Peter/Animals Animals/Earth
    Scenes, 31
PhotoDisc, 25, 29 (top, middle), 37
©Jeffrey L. Rottman/CORBIS, 21
Suzanne Santillan, 9, 12, 14, 17, 22, 34

About the Author

Bonnie Juettner is a writer and editor of children's reference books and educational videos. Originally from McGrath, Alaska, she currently lives in Kenosha, Wisconsin. This is her fourth book.